THE DARK DARK KNIGHT

Lesley Sims
Illustrated by Peter Wingham

Designed by Lucy Smith
Series Editor: Gaby Waters

Contents

The Prophecy

Welcome friend. I am Nerlym the Enchanter. The tale you are about to read began many centuries ago in a kingdom called Hamalot. Watch the story unfold in the smoke from my fire.

The kingdom of Hamalot was ruled by Good King Stan. It wasn't an easy job. King Stan had to spend most of his time fighting off fiendish beasts.

These beasts were servants of a villain known as the Dark Dark Knight. Tales of his wickedness were many but no one had ever seen him. He gave orders through an evil witch called Nastina.

Thurs 3pm:
Grand Battle
between
Good King Stan &
the Dark Dark
Knight!

Daily the Dark Dark Knight's powers grew stronger. Finally King Stan was challenged to a battle to decide the fate of the kingdom.

But just before the battle was due to begin, three of King Stan's most loyal knights vanished.

King Stan was captured, and held prisoner by an evil spell in Nastina's Tower of Desolation.

As the King was captured, milk curdled, toast burned and a violent storm began. Everyone waited in terror for the Dark Dark Knight to begin his reign.

Finally, the frightened people of Hamalot fled their towns and came to the castle to consult my Special Book of Knowledge.

Ye Special Book of Knowledge
Chapter 7 : Ye Prophecy

Lo there shall be a time when fear hangs a black cloud over ye land.

Then shall appear two saviours, St Halo and ye Martyr.

These Heroines shall descend from ye heavens seeking King Stan to save them from a darke, darke nighte.

Despite greate peril they shall undertake ye quest for King Stan.

The people were very relieved.

But I must stop talking and let you find out what happened next. As the tale continues, maybe you can solve the puzzles and unravel the mystery of the Dark Dark Knight.

The Haunted Wood

A thousand years after King Stan was captured, two friends called Haley and Martha were standing where the battle should have been fought . . . in Haley's kitchen.

They were taking a picnic to Yew Tree Wood. It had been growing wild for centuries and there were lots of creepy stories about it. Some even said the wood was haunted by ancient tree spirits.

Suddenly the radio crackled into life with a newsflash.

. . . very odd things have been happening. All the money in the town bank has turned to dough, the library books have become moths and the local museum has been ransacked. Now with the time at ten past nine we . . .

"Come on! Let's go or we'll miss the bus!" said Haley. Outside a fierce wind had sprung up from nowhere.

As they ran for the bus stop past the bank, a gust of wind blew a piece of paper straight into Haley's hand.

This is all my doing. Worse is to come until I find what I seek. You have been warned!

The Dark Dark Knight ...

On the bus she showed it to Martha. It was a note but it didn't seem to mean anything. They didn't even know who it was for, so Haley threw it away with her ticket. Just then the bus reached the wood and they jumped off, the odd note forgotten.

The wood was gloomier than normal as they hurried to their usual spot. But somehow, without noticing, they must have taken a wrong turn.

All of a sudden they were in a strange, unknown part of the wood, completely lost.

Then Martha spotted something behind a tangle of brambles. It was a door! Martha tried the handle but it was locked. A breeze rustled the leaves above her. "Key," they seemed to whisper.

Can you see a key?

5

Carved in Stone

Martha reached up for the key. But as she held it in her hand, the brambles parted as if by magic. Then slowly the door creaked open. Nervously they entered.

Inside was a chapel, eerily quiet. A stone tomb rose before them, bearing two lifelike figures of sleeping knights. A candle beside the tomb lit up a strange message on its base.

Haley tried to read it but it seemed to be in some ancient language. Then she realized it was in code and began to decipher the inscription.

She read it in amazement. Meanwhile Martha had found a horn hanging from a pillar. "WAIT!" Haley shouted. She was too late. Martha blew it.

What does the message say?

The Statues Awake

The walls began to shake and dust clouds filled the air. Martha and Haley watched in amazement as the two stone figures began to move.

They were stretching and sitting up. Haley and Martha stared in stunned silence.

The two stone knights, who weren't stone at all, stood up and brushed dust from their chainmail. The larger one glared at Martha. "Hey!" he said. "Where's the battle?"

"B-battle? W-what battle?" asked Martha in shock.

"The great one of course, against the villainous Dark Dark Knight," he said. The girls looked blank. "The whole of the kingdom's at stake," he added.

Then he noticed the inscription. "Hey Sir Roy, listen to this!" he said to the skinny knight, who was jumping around fighting a duel with the air.

"Treachery!" the skinny knight shouted. "What year is it then?" Haley answered automatically.

"Nineteen ninety what?" yelled the knight. "So who won the battle?" He paused and shuddered. "You don't suppose the Dark Dark Knight . . ?"

Haley and Martha didn't have a clue what was going on, but the Dark Dark Knight was the name on the note they'd thrown away in the bus.

"He must be stopped," said Sir Roy. "We have to get back to King Stan somehow. We MUST go to the castle!" he declared.

"There's no castle near here," said Martha, vaguely remembering a King Stan from her history book.

"Yes there is!" said Sir Roy and he began to describe the castle and its surrounding landmarks.

"Maybe there was a castle here once," said Haley, fishing a map from her bag and listening to the knight's description.

Where do you think the castle was?

It's a magnificent sight. A river runs to the east. Northeast are the famous Awlup Hills. A monastery lies directly to the south. It's just inside the City Walls. You must know it.

MAP OF STANTON
FREE
WITH EVERY BURGER!

N

STATION

AWLUP HILLS HOSPITAL

BARON WAISTE INDUSTRIES

TOWN HALL

MUSEUM

CASTLE CINEMA

TOWN SQUARE

BOATING LAKE

SHOPPING MALL

BURGER BAR

POST OFFICE

BANK

BUS STATION

LEISURE PARK WITH MONSTER MAZE

BULLFIELD HOUSING ESTATE

MONKS PARK

PITT FOREST SCHOOL

TOLL

BRIDGE

KEY
RAILWAY
RIVER
SITE OF RUIN
ANCIENT CITY WALL

CASTLE HOTEL

UNDERGROUND CAR PARK

Hamalot's Burger Bar

Ten minutes later, they were at the site of the old castle, which was now Hamalot's Burger Bar (fast food with a medieval theme).

The knights were still with them and they weren't interested in hamburgers, they just wanted King Stan. All of a sudden a man came out of the kitchen. He was wearing a funny costume like the man behind the till.

But to the girls' surprise he raised his arms and greeted the knights like a long lost friend.

"Sir Roy! Sir Simon!" he cried. "What are you doing here?"

"Sir Percy?" exclaimed Sir Simon, the larger knight. He beamed at the man. "We've come to the castle but it seems to have gone."

He saw Martha and Haley's puzzled faces. "This is Sir Percy, the Knight Watchman and Keeper of Time," Sir Simon explained.

"Shh! I'm here undercover," Sir Percy said. "I wondered what had happened to you. Just after you vanished King Stan was captured," he told them. The knights gasped in disbelief. "You two must go back," he added.

"Use my Timedial," he said, giving Sir Roy a locket from his belt. "Say when and where you want to go, turn the pointer to the T factor and press the button. You can only go back, not forward and it will only work twice. I must go or I'll blow my cover."

Haley and Martha stared at him open-mouthed. Things were getting weirder by the minute.

The locket or Timedial turned out to be a pocket sundial, with instructions on the lid. Sir Roy read them quickly.

"Hamalot Castle, just after the battle," he gabbled, setting the pointer to three. He hit the button and the Timedial flew through the air. Haley caught it worriedly. She didn't think three was the answer.

Is three the right number?

To find the T factor:
Multiply the number of people going back by 6, if the number of people is 3 or less, or by 9 if the number is more than 3. Then subtract one third. If the answer is more than one digit, add them together until you have a single digit answer.

11

The Quest

There was a flash. Haley and Martha blinked. Hamalot's had gone. Instead they were in a blue room staring into the face of an old man with a long beard.

Behind them a man gave a shout. "The Heroines!" he said in awed tones and bowed. With a start the girls realized he meant them. Then the old man spoke.

"I am Nerlym the Enchanter," he said. "Welcome to Hamalot St. Halo and the Martyr."

"St. Halo and WHO?" said Martha. "I think you're confusing us with someone else!"

Nerlym shook his head. "We've been expecting you," he said. The girls were speechless.

"This is the Blue Briefing Room, inner sanctum of King Stan's loyal Knights of the Little Oval Table," Nerlym added. "We're planning your Quest to rescue King Stan."

The girls were horrified. Then Nerlym told them a tale of a dastardly knight and how only King Stan could defeat him.

After his story three things were clear. They'd gone back in time. They had to go on some quest – alone. Worst of all they couldn't go home until they had.

"This is about the Quest but in ancient Chivalric I'm afraid," said Nerlym, unfurling a scroll. It looked like an easy code. **Can you decipher the message?**

If we were meet to go, the Book would have said.

Good point!

THEQRIC UESTRIC
FORKRIC INGSRIC TANRIC

STHA LOMA RTDYRRIC THISRIC
YOURRIC QUESRIC TTOFRIC
REENRIC ASTI NASCRIC APTU
REDGRIC UESTRIC FIRSRIC TYOU
MUSTRIC FINDRIC TWOCRIC
HAINRIC MAILRIC VESTRIC
SASTRIC ARRYRIC SWORRIC
DANDRIC SHTE LDSTRIC HENSRIC
EEKWRIC ISEMRIC ONKSRIC
WHOLRIC LTELRIC LYOU MORE
OFHO WTORRIC EACHRIC NASTRIC
INASRIC DOORRIC YOURRIC SHTE
LDSWRIC ILLHRIC ELPTRIC OCRO
SSHE RFLO ORANRIC DTHE
NHERRIC FATE ISSE ALEDRIC.

A Broken Sword

Nerlym gave them the scroll and led them outside. "Good luck!" he said. "By the way, Nastina only has power over three things. Anything else is illusion."

"What three things?" said Haley but Nerlym had gone. They were left, puzzled and alone, and all they had to go on was a confusing rhyme on a scroll.

Martha shrugged. "I suppose we'd better find shields and this chainmail," she said. "But where from?" The only person in sight was a gardener who seemed to be weeding. Perhaps he could help.

To their surprise, he was nibbling leaves. "You need Sir John, the swordsmith. Seee Sirrrr Johhhhn," he bleated.

He shook his head and his hair stood up in two pointed tufts. Were they imagining things? Could he be growing horns?

Martha and Haley stared in horror. He was definitely changing shape! As they stood bemused, he butted Haley onto a different path.

"A goat?!" she said to Martha spinning around. There in front of them was a hut. "Er, we need Sir John," she called to a knight in the doorway.

"That's me!" he said.

"The, er, gardener told us to see you," said Martha.

"Barry the Weregoat?" said Sir John. "He's harmless. Come in!"

Sir John found them tunics and two shields with cryptic messages he couldn't explain.

"Now, swords," said Sir John. "They're handmade and there's a six-week waiting list." He pointed to a heap of old metal on the floor. "You could look there."

"We can't make a sword out of pieces like a jigsaw!" said Martha.

"You might," Sir John grinned. **Which of the sword pieces fit together to make one sword?**

Follow that Monk!

Sir John smiled as the last piece of sword was put in place. To the girls' surprise it glowed and sprang together like new.

"Now we need to find these wise monks," said Martha, reading the scroll and as luck would have it, there outside the hut were two.

Martha grinned. "We can follow them," she said to Haley as the monks set off. "This Quest isn't so hard after all!"

They walked on and on until it felt like they'd been walking forever. But at last they arrived at the monastery.

"We're on a Quest to rescue King Stan," said Haley showing a monk the scroll. "We've come to ask what to do next."

First pass the entrance test!

A Little Knowledge is a Dangerous Thing! How Much do you Know? Enough to be Let in?

He sent them to the library where they were stopped by a second monk who pointed to a sign over the door.

"A test? This is like school," said Martha. The monk frowned and gave Haley a piece of parchment and an inky quill.

As Haley studied the parchment, Martha read the questions over her shoulder. "This is just like a puzzle book," Haley groaned. **Can you solve the quiz?**

BROTHER BEN'S BRAINTEASERS

1. Fill in the missing values

			39
			?
			?
25	?	31	?

2. Add the bell and candle

3. Find the Fiends!

D	W	B	H	A	G	I	L
E	R	E	T	S	N	O	M
R	D	A	F	R	T	G	F
I	W	S	G	N	O	R	T
P	A	T	A	O	A	L	C
M	R	I	G	W	N	V	L
A	G	R	D	F	H	A	B
V	E	R	T	C	E	P	S

Can you strike out all ten fiends hidden in the grid? (They are listed around the edge of the parchment.)

4. The Pilgrims' Progress

Two pilgrims set out from shrines in nearby towns. Each is visiting the shrine the other has just left. They travel at exactly the same speed, yet one takes 1 hour and 20 minutes to arrive, while the other reaches his shrine in only 80 minutes. How?

MONSTER
GIANT OGRE DWARF
HAG
BEAST
VAMPIRE
DRAGON
SPECTRE   TROLL

Books and Clues

With a stern "Be quiet in there," they were let in. Inside sat row upon row of hooded figures, all bent over high desks. Each was painstakingly copying a manuscript. A monk came up to Martha.

"We're on a quest," she said. "We need to know how to get to Nastina's Tower." Haley rustled the scroll. "Ssshhh!" came a dozen voices from behind.

The monk glanced at the scroll and disappeared. Soon he was back with an old book called Tall Tales, stuffed full of papers and dried flowers.

A jumble of papers? How would they help? Haley felt confused. Then she realized that if they pieced together all the information from the papers and put it into the right order, they would know what to do next.

Where should they go first?

Brother Gregory's Alphabet Chant

An exercise to warm up the voice

a e i o u   b c d g   m n   p q r s t

Madrigal for Monk and Pipes*

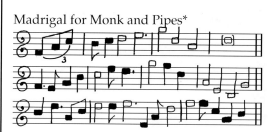

*It's best to use pipes made by Herman. His pipes even hypnotize the ferocious dragon Phaal. The pipes cannot be bought but Herman will exchange one for the rare scented Hytee leaves from Araby.

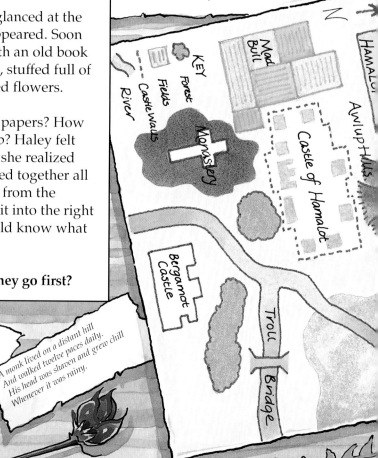

A monk sat on the cloister steps.
A wind blew from the East.
"I'll have to go," he sadly said,
"I've missed the winter feast."

A monk lived on a distant hill
And walked twelve paces daily.
His head was shaven and grew chill
Whenever it was rainy.

CLOISTERS CHRONICLE

KING KIDNAPPED!
by Brother Dan

Good King Stan has been the victim of a terrible trick and is now held prisoner in the grim Tower of Desolation.

As the Great Battle against the Dark Dark Knight was about to begin, three loyal KLOTs were spirited away and King Stan was grabbed by Nastina's Nasties.

Each day King Stan is away, the power of the Dark Dark Knight grows stronger. Any day now he will arrive to take control.

Learn to read & write in 5 days! For further details write to The Monastery.

GRAND FAYRE

This was a huge success with a record crowd of 57, two pigs and a goat. The winner of the Beautiful Turnip competition was Nag Miggins. Well done Nag!

The Wandring Minstrels
at the village inn.
Doors open at 4pm.

To release a knight from evil enchantment call his name three times.

Monastery Rhymes
A funky monk picked up his lute
And sang a little song;
Ten other monks threw rotten fruit
Each note he plucked was wrong:

Tall Tales: The Towers of Hamalot

The Tower of Desolation

The Tower of Desolation lies in the middle of the Barren Wastes and is home to the evil Nastina.

Though there is no doubt it exists, no one has a clear idea of what it looks like because it is usually invisible.

The Tower is defended by three ingenious but invisible obstacles. Each one must be overcome before the next one will appear.

The door to the Tower is

An artist's impression of the Tower of Desolation

blocked by Silverkeys the Guardian. He is protected by Three Crones who in turn are guarded by the dragon Phaal.

Phaal and the three crones

Phaal lives in a devious labyrinth. Though immortal, he can be hypnotized. Until he's defeated, the exit to the Crones is hidden.

In Deep Trouble

First they had to visit Earl Grey for Hytee leaves. It wasn't far to go but it was getting dark, so the monks invited them to stay.

This is our best room. Sleep well!

At sunrise they set off. Soon they were on the edge of a great forest. But before long Martha was moaning. Her feet hurt.

"What we need is a horse," she said. No sooner than she had spoken, and to her immense surprise, a horse appeared from behind some trees.

"This is weird!" cried Martha leaping astride the horse. It swung around and charged back into the forest. Haley just managed to jump on as Martha shot past.

A terrifying ten-minute ride followed. They clung to the horse's mane as it galloped over bushes, under branches and around trees at high speed. Then it stopped – so abruptly that the girls flew over its head into a deep pit.

"Gotcha!" bellowed a voice. Martha and Haley looked up to see a hideous creature above them.

"Ha! New servants for me cookings and me cleanings," it said. "Stay there till I needs you."

Haley and Martha climbed to their feet, relieved to find they had no broken bones.

"What next?" said Haley crossly, looking at the leering creature. "He looks like he's escaped from a fairy tale."

Martha didn't hear. She'd seen a stone slab propped against the pit wall with three sentences on it. She read the first one out.

"Ha! Them's me riddles," said the creature. "If you gets them right I might let you go . . ."

Martha grinned. "They're just anagrams. That's easy!" she said and reeled off the answers.

". . . then again I might not," the creature added grumpily.

"I wish I'd never jumped on that horse," said Martha.

When Haley fell she'd landed on something hard in her pocket. She felt it curiously. "That's it!" she cried. "We can easily get out!"

What is Haley's escape plan?

Arabian Knights

In a flash they were back on the edge of the forest. This time they ignored the horse and ran on. Half an hour later they reached a river. Earl Grey's castle stood on the opposite bank.

Some time later, they squelched up a long drive, under a vast gateway and in through the main doors.

Prince Coriander, who doesn't wear yellow, brought gems.

The knight wearing blue came by elephant.

Neither Sir Nutmeg nor the knight in green came by elephant.

They had stepped straight into a Great Hall. There were tables full of magnificent food but it was all growing cold. To their surprise a round, fat man smiled as they entered.

"Welcome!" he cried. "At last we can eat. Name your challenge strangers!" Martha and Haley were puzzled.

"It's an old rule," said the man. "We can't begin our feast until a puzzle or problem has been solved. How can we help? Are you damsels in distress?"

"Not really," said Haley. "We need Hytee leaves from Araby."

"Ha!" cried the man. "Then I shall set you a puzzle. The four royal knights on my right are from Araby. But which one has the Hytee leaves? If you can't guess you'll be sent to the dungeons for a year and a day."

To Martha and Haley's relief, hungry guests shouted clues. Soon they could identify each knight, say what he had brought and how he'd arrived.

Which knight has the Hytee leaves?

Underground Secrets

They were given a tiny packet, which Haley put in her pocket, and they set out again. The landscape grew bleak. After a while they reached a fork in the track. "Which way now?" said Martha. "This wasn't on the map."

"Look, we can ask him!" said Haley, pointing to a figure in the distance. But something about the way he approached, bent over and hurrying, made them hesitate.

As he passed they saw his crest – the same as the one on the note. Was he one of the Dark Dark Knight's men? They had to find out.

A pair of giant rocks loomed ahead. The man slipped between them and vanished. Silently, they followed him.

They climbed down some steps and found themselves in a passageway. The man was in a brightly-lit chamber.

They hid by the doorway and watched him. He was reading a letter. Then he tore it up, threw it on the fire and hurried to the doorway.

Haley and Martha dashed back up the stairs around a corner and held their breath. To their huge relief, the man rushed off in the opposite direction. They waited for a few seconds and then ran into the room.

Martha quickly snatched up a poker to retrieve the fragments of letter. Luckily they had fallen onto the grate and the fire had hardly touched them.

Haley looked at one of the fragments and gasped. "It's from the Dark Dark Knight," she said. "If we can put it back together, we might learn more about him!"

What does the letter say?

To my faithful page, Fred –
I expect you are wondering
a week ago. When will I return
patient. The time has come to
memorize this letter, then
I have spent many years
legend of the Moon Goblet.
he who uses it to drink water
moon's reflection in it, shall be
invincible. Those foolish KLOTs
Goblet is a legend. I have proof

Nerlym's father. He feared its
future. But I have found it! I
a flashing box. When I have
me and my reign will last
Goblet _must_ be used on All
away. I called the battle too soon.
those dratted Heroines have turned
Roy with them). Go straight to

Yours hurriedly,
Dark Dark Knight

It was made in the time of
power and threw it far into the
even took a picture of it with
drunk from it no one will stop
... forever! I made one error. The
Ghouls' Eve, still a few days
Now time is short. Already
up (and brought Simon and
Nastina and tell her.

The

where I've been since the battle
to claim my throne? Soon. Be
reveal my masterplan. Read and
studying the
This says that
with the
immortal and
think the
it exists!

DESTROY IT!

Troll Toll

It was hard to imagine how much power the Dark Dark Knight would wield if his plan succeeded. But they knew one thing. He had to be stopped. Haley ran to the steps.

"Wait!" said Martha pulling her back. "That man was going to Nastina's tower too. We'll be quicker if we follow him."

The steps led to a tunnel. Martha scrambled along. Haley followed, noticing some paper on the ground. Martha must have dropped it in her haste, she thought and pocketed it.

Past the tunnel, the way ahead was blocked by a river. They were about to cross the bridge when something jumped out at them.

"This is a troll toll bridge," it said. "I'm the troll! You have to pay me a toll before you cross."

"If you can't pay, you'll have to fight my knight," it added and gave a piercing whistle.

A strange-looking knight appeared before them. He was huge and silent and his eyes were glazed over, as if he wasn't seeing anything. He didn't react to them at all, just walked slowly and silently in their direction.

He grasped Haley's shoulder and led her to a horse. She tried to wriggle free but his grip was unshakable. Then he gave her a lance. He seemed oblivious to the fact that she was half his size and not even a knight.

Martha watched in horror. There was no way Haley could win. Something else about the knight bothered Martha, apart from the fact that he was in league with a horrible warty troll.

As the knight mounted his horse, Martha recognized his coat of arms. Of course! He was a KLOT. But how could she stop him? Then it dawned on her – he'd been enchanted. She'd read in the library that to call his name three times would break the spell. But what was his name?

Do you know?

Herman the Hermit

Martha called his name and Sir Gavin awoke. The girls raced across the bridge chased by the troll. Sir Gavin raced after the troll and chased it away.

"Only me!" said a voice unhelpfully. "I was divining."

The mist began to lift and they saw the owner of the voice.

"I'm Herman," he grinned and gave a little bow.

It was Herman the Hermit, the maker of pipes. Haley told him about their quest. The leaves were very crushed but Herman didn't seem to mind. "Hytee leaves for me? Splendid!" he said.

His hut was cramped and smelled damp. He hunted for the pipe, chattering to himself. "Visitors! Makes a change. I don't see anyone now Nastina's next door. Who wants to be near her?"

"Even if her Tower's invisible," he went on. "That's just her tricksy magic that is. You only see it when you break through the other obstacles. Aha!" he cried at last, waving a pipe and some music.

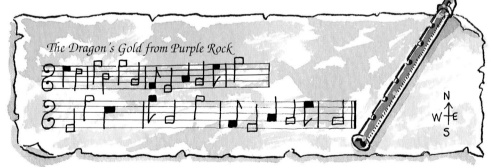

The Dragon's Gold from Purple Rock

"The problem," he added, "is that my pipes only hypnotize the dragon if you can find him. I've spent years hunting, even bought music from a door-to-door minstrel who promised it would lead me to him. But I sat on the Purple Rock and played it. Nothing happened."

"Suppose it's not music at all," said Haley slowly, studying it. She'd seen some like it recently. "I think it's coded directions made to look like music. The Purple Rock is where we start from."

Where should they go?

The Labyrinth

By a red rock Haley took out the pipe and blew it. Nothing happened. Meanwhile Martha was excitedly reading two pieces of paper which had fallen out of Haley's pocket.

"You dropped them," Haley said. But they weren't Martha's.

Fred,
You must feed Phaal. If I leave the Tower, my hold over Stan is weakened. Go to the Red Rock and say, "Mighty Nastina, she who commands serpents, stone and steel, now bids you answer her demand: the dragon's lair reveal!" You will find yourself where I have marked 'X' on this plan. Nastina

They were a note from Nastina and a plan of the labyrinth. Martha recited the rhyme on the note, then . . . did they sink or did the ground rise up? Suddenly they were in a high-walled tunnel, open to the sky. The only way out was to find the middle, for Phaal guarded the exit at the maze's heart.

What is the route to Phaal?

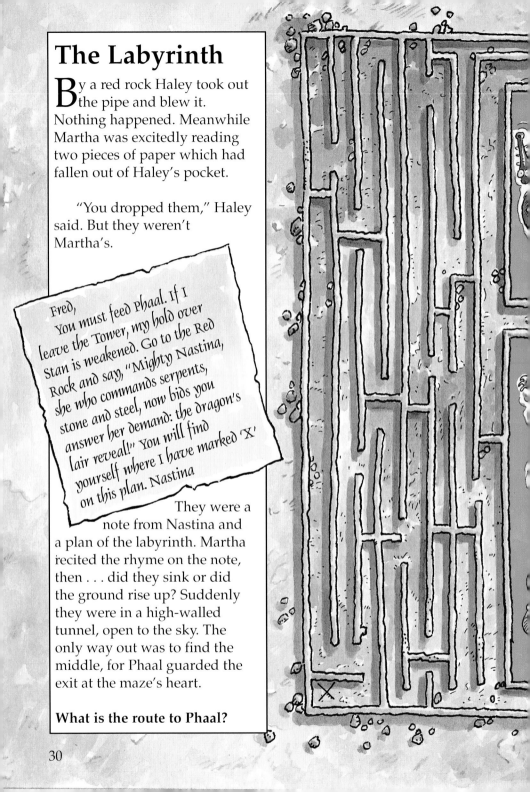

30

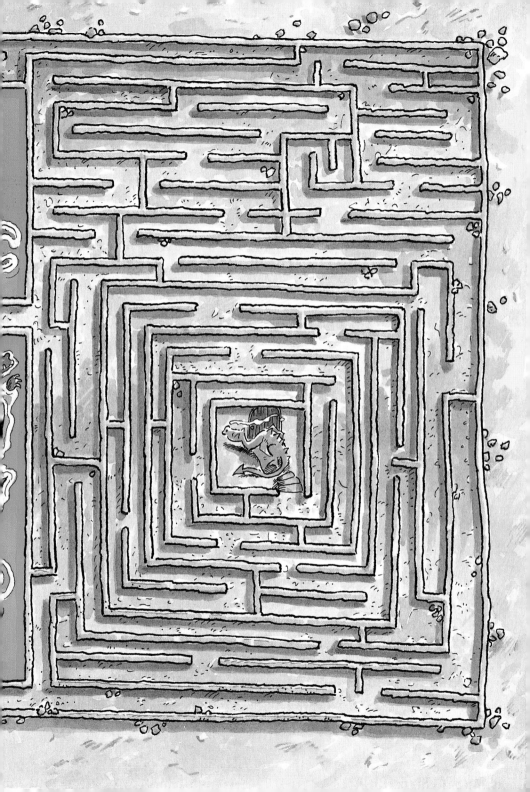

A Dragon and Three Crones

At last they reached the steps which led down to Phaal. The gaping mouth of a cave grew bigger and darker as they went closer. It glowed a deep red. Red? thought Haley. How odd.

"GET OUT! It's his mouth!" cried Martha. "Quick, the pipe!"

They leapt back as Phaal reared up before them. Haley's mouth felt dry but she stuck the pipe in and blew. A few quavery notes came out. They sounded terrible.

Phaal paused. Martha shut her eyes fearing the worst. But Haley played some more, slowly moving the pipe from side to side, like a snake charmer.

Phaal followed the pipe, from left to right to left. Slowly his eyes closed and he sank down onto his huge pile of treasure. A rumbling snore told them he was asleep.

Now they could see daylight coming into the labyrinth through three holes in the far wall.

Martha led the way over Phaal's treasure to the first exit. But an old woman blocked the way out.

"I cannot see to let you pass. Find my specs or stay stuck fast," she cackled.

At the second exit an even older, uglier hag stopped them.

"You want to leave? You'll have to shout. With my hearing trumpet I'd let you out," she bellowed.

At the last exit was the ugliest crone of all. "Wiffout my teef I cannot chew. If I faint from hunger, you won't get frew," she gabbled. "And only one of free won't do," she added cryptically.

Haley and Martha looked at her, puzzled. One of free? "Oh, three!" said Haley. "We have to find their three things to get out of here. We'd better find them fast before he wakes up," she added.

Martha looked at the sleeping dragon. "I hope they're not underneath him," she whispered.

Can you find the crones' missing things?

Guardian of the Tower

The three crones grasped their things and turned away, gloating. Haley and Martha slipped through the third exit.

Outside, they stopped and stared in amazement. Half shrouded in mists, a ghostly wall was growing before them.

A misty tower rose up behind the wall. Gradually, the mist took on a more solid look.

Then a door studded with spikes appeared. Haley touched it cautiously. It felt real enough. Gripping the sword, she opened the door and they went in.

They found themselves in a courtyard paved in black and white. A small man with several keys jangling on his belt came up to them.

"So you got past Phaal and his fair maidens," he said with an evil laugh. "You won't defeat me. There's only one route to the Tower. Step on the wrong stone at the wrong time and . . ."

He threw a twig onto a black square. The twig fizzed and then dissolved, running down between the cracks in the stones.

"Only the white squares with flags are always safe," he said. He pointed to a sundial. "If you reach the door before twelve, I'll unlock it. If not, and you're still alive, you'll be left to rot in the dungeons."

Martha gulped. The shadow was almost at twelve now. What could they do? Then a line from the scroll ran through her mind.

Your shields help to cross her floor. Martha studied the shields. "That's it!" she said. "The lines on your shield show which way we go, north, south, east or west. The symbols on my shield show how many squares we cross each time. I have two green trees, so whenever you have a green line, we cross two squares. Your first line is green and points north, so we go two squares north. Follow me!"

Can you find a route to the door?

Inside the Tower

The tower door slammed shut behind them. "You won't find it so easy to get out," snarled the man from outside.

Haley and Martha looked around. They were in a small, dimly-lit hallway which was almost filled by a spiral staircase.

Martha took a deep breath and started to climb. Warily, Haley followed her.

Darkened rooms led off the stairs. The girls peered around half-closed doors, each time terrified that one would open on Nastina, evil mistress of the tower.

Finally they found a brightly decorated room. A smiling knight called to them. Was this King Stan?

Haley felt uneasy. The figure didn't seem real. Martha was going in when Haley held her back. "Wait!" she said.

As she spoke, the knight and the room vanished. They were left teetering on the brink of a gaping hole. Haley hauled Martha back from the edge just in time.

Terrified, they climbed higher finally reaching the top of the tower. A dazed knight was slumped in the corner of a room at the end of the staircase.

He didn't even look up as they came in. "King Stan?" said Haley. The knight groaned. "Help me get him up," Haley said to Martha. "We must get him out of here."

"I don't think so," said a rasping voice behind them. Nastina stood in the doorway, her arms raised above her head, lightning flashing from her fingers.

She entered and the doorway vanished. Thunderbolts shook the room as four new doorways sprang up. Each revealed a deadly trap.

"Exits of spider, serpents, stone and steel," laughed Nastina. "But dare you use them? You can only go through one anyway," she said and vanished.

Haley frowned. Suddenly she remembered Nerlym's last words to them. Then she thought of the rhyme that made the labyrinth appear. She smiled. One doorway was safe.

Which one is it?

A Call to Arms

As soon as Haley stepped into the web, it vanished. They dragged the dopey King down the spiral staircase. Once outside, he quickly revived.

"Into battle!" he cried and then stopped. "Where am I? Who are you? What's going on?" he asked.

"No time to explain," Martha panted. "We must go to Hamalot now. I hope we're not too late."

"We'll be there in a trice!" said King Stan, clicking his fingers. "To Hamalot!" he cried. And quicker than a blink they were there.

"Sire! Heroines!" cried Nerlym. "I'd almost given up hope. The Dark Dark Knight is still missing but something is afoot. He's bound to be plotting something terrible. If only I knew what . . . "

"He wants to be invincible," said Martha. "He's after some goblet and I think he's found it." Nerlym gasped. "I'm sure I've seen it somewhere," Martha muttered to herself. "But where?"

"We must find it first," King Stan declared. "Call my KLOTs. Tell them to prepare for battle!"

"They're all over the castle," said Nerlym. "It will take me all afternoon to find them. But I won't mention a battle or they won't come. I'll just say the king is free!"

Nerlym hurried away. The knights were enjoying a free afternoon but finally nearly everyone was gathered in the Hall.

"The Dark Dark Knight will threaten us no more!" King Stan declared. The knights cheered. "We leave now for the final battle!" he added. The knights began to make excuses.

"We shall all leave now for . . . er, where are we going?" said King Stan. In a flash Martha remembered where she'd seen the goblet before.

Do you?

The Last Battle of All

King Stan clicked his fingers. Instantly the castle became the burger bar but the goblet had gone. Outside Haley saw a dark figure by the water fountain.

Everyone ran to the fountain. A knight in black was watching the moon's reflection on the water's surface. With a triumphant cry he scooped up the reflection.

"STOP!" cried King Stan rushing up to him and knocking the goblet from the knight's hand.

A desperate duel began. At first the knights cheered but they soon fell silent.

The Dark Dark Knight was winning. He flicked King Stan's sword from his hand.

Look, the sword's gone through his mask!

That's got him! Scratch his face!

Haley quickly handed King Stan her sword. Sparks flashed like stars as it left the scabbard. Slowly the tables were turned.

At last the Dark Dark Knight was pinned against the fountain, the sword at his throat. King Stan was about to unmask him when . . .

. . . clouds of black smoke surrounded them, leaving everyone choking. When the smoke cleared the Dark Dark Knight had gone.

The knights looked at each other in dismay. "The villain has escaped!" said King Stan in horror. Haley and Martha looked around. He was no longer the Dark Dark Knight but he hadn't gone far. They knew where he was.

Do you?

41

A Dark Knight Ends

How dare you accuse ME, Sir Jack Upall!

"It's him!" cried Haley, pointing. King Stan refused to believe her. It couldn't be one of his KLOTs.

"We can prove it!" said Martha. "The Dark Dark Knight wrote a letter to his servant Fred telling him all about us. Only Nerlym and the KLOTs knew we'd arrived."

"When we left Hamalot castle there was one knight missing," Haley added. "But now all the KLOTs are here. If you want any more proof, look at his cheek. It was grazed in the duel."

King Stan told the knight to remove his mask. There on his cheek was a trickle of dried blood. "Grab him!" ordered King Stan.

He turned to Haley and Martha. "Thank you for all your help. Now we must return to our own time before any more harm is done."

He clicked his fingers, there was a flash and then King Stan, his knights and Nerlym had gone. Haley and Martha were alone.

"Let's go home," Martha said after a few seconds. "I want to check my old history book. Do you think it describes King Stan and his glorious rescue by Saint Halo and the Martyr?"

Clues

Pages 4-5
Keys don't grow on trees . . . do they?

Pages 6-7
Each word has been reversed and an extra letter added in front. The extra letters also hide a message.

Pages 8-9
Some landmarks may have changed over the centuries.

Pages 10-11
Sir Roy used 9 in his sum, yet only he and Sir Simon were going back.

Pages 12-13
Chivalric breaks up words into groups of four and adds three letters to all words not ending in a vowel.

Pages 14-15
Fit the pieces of sword together. There are pieces for more than one sword.

Pages 16-17
1. Find the value of the jug first.
2. The bell and candle move around in a sequence.
3. Read up, down, diagonally and from side to side.
4. How many minutes in 1 hour, 20 minutes?

Pages 18-19
Start with the Tower of Desolation and work back.

Pages 20-21
Solving the anagrams didn't help Martha, but something she said has given Haley an idea.

Pages 22-23
Using what you know you can fill in the gaps. As Coriander didn't ride the camel or horse he must have come by elephant or mule. But he brought gems and the mule carried wooden things. So Coriander rode the elephant and is the knight in blue.

Pages 24-25
Trace the pieces and fit them together.

Pages 26-27
A KLOT was missing when they arrived. Check the shields on page 12.

Pages 28-29
The alphabet chant in the library gives each note a letter.

Pages 30-31
Watch out for blind alleys.

Pages 32-33
Search the treasure carefully.

Pages 34-35
A red line means one square, a green line means two squares and a blue line means three squares.

Pages 36-37
The rhyme tells you which three things Nastina has power over.

Pages 38-39
Martha must have seen the Moon Goblet before they went back in time.

Pages 40-41
The Dark Dark Knight has gone but another knight has arrived. Who is he?

Answers

Pages 4-5

The key is circled below.

Pages 6-7

Each word has been written back to front and begins with an extra letter. With the letters in the right order, the inscription reads:

Here lie two most puny knights, the KLOTs Sir Simon and Sir Roy. I cast a spell on these two knights and transported them here in a deep sleep. In this chapel they shall sleep forever, unless someone is clever enough to decipher this message and wake them. The Horn of Awakening will rouse them. Blow it if you dare . . .   Nastina AD995

The extra letters also make a sentence: Don't meddle with things you don't understand. You will live to regret it! N

Pages 8-9

If you match the descriptions of the old landmarks to the places shown on the modern map, you will see that Hamalot's Burger Bar stands on the site of Stan's castle. The three hills are now the Awlup Hills Hospital.

Pages 10-11

The right number was 8. Sir Roy should have multiplied 2 (him and Sir Simon) by 6. Instead he multiplied 2 by 9 = 18, less a third = 12 and then added 2 and 1 together.

3 was completely wrong. It's surprising the Timedial worked at all. Perhaps someone was watching to help the Prophecy come true.

Pages 12-13

Chivalric breaks up words into groups of four and adds "ric" to the end of every group not finishing with a vowel. Decoded the scroll reads:

The Quest for King Stan

St. Halo, Martyr,
this your Quest:
To free Nastina's captured guest.
First you must find two
chainmail vests,
A starry sword and shields.
Then seek wise monks
who'll tell you more
Of how to reach Nastina's door.
Your shields will help
to cross her floor
And then her fate is sealed.

Pages 14-15

The pieces they need have been circled.

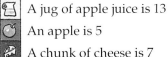

The sword fits together like this:

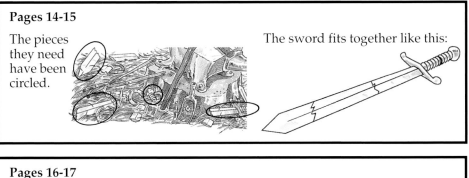

Pages 16-17

1. Missing values

A jug of apple juice is 13

An apple is 5

A chunk of cheese is 7

2. Bell and candle

3. Find the Fiends

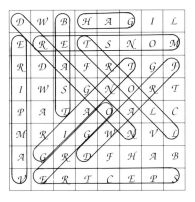

4. Pilgrims' Progress

One hour 20 minutes is the same as 80 minutes.

Pages 18-19

To enter the Tower of Desolation Haley and Martha must first defeat Silverkeys the Guardian of the Tower. They learn this from the book "Tall Tales." The book also tells them that to reach Silverkeys, they must get past the Three Crones – who can't be reached without finding and defeating Phaal the dragon.

The sheet of music tells them that Phaal can be hypnotized with one of Herman's pipes and that he will swap a pipe for Hytee leaves from Araby.

An advertisement in the newspaper says that Earl Grey imports spices and leaves from Araby, so Bergamot Castle is where they should start.

Pages 20-21

Haley still has Sir Percy's Timedial. Her plan is to go back in time to just before they saw the horse and then ignore it.

(The three anagrams are magician, sword and adventure.)

Pages 22-23

Duke Turmeric who wears red and rode a camel, brought the Hytee leaves.

Prince Coriander wears blue, came by elephant and brought gems.

Sir Nutmeg wears yellow and rode a mule carrying the carved wooden things.

Lord Fenugreek wears green, rode a horse and brought perfume.

Pages 24-25

When the letter is pieced together, this is what it says:

To my faithful page, Fred —

   I expect you are wondering where I've been since the battle a week ago. When will I return to claim my throne? Soon. Be patient. The time has come to reveal my masterplan. Read and memorize this letter, then DESTROY IT!

   I have spent many years studying the legend of the Moon Goblet. This says that he who uses it to drink water with the moon's reflection in it, shall be immortal and invincible. Those foolish KLOTs think the Goblet is a legend. I have proof it exists!

   It was made in the time of Nerlym's father. He feared its power and threw it far into the future. But I have found it! I even took a picture of it with a flashing box. When I have drunk from it no one will stop me and my reign will last forever! I made one error. The Goblet must be used on All Ghouls' Eve, still a few days away. I called the battle too soon. Now time is short. Already those dratted Heroines have turned up (and brought Simon and Roy with them). Go straight to Nastina and tell her.

                    Yours hurriedly,
                    The Dark Dark Knight

Pages 26-27

He is Sir Gavin Goode. He was enchanted by Nastina at the same time as Sir Simon and Sir Roy, and given to the troll.

Pages 28-29

The music can be translated using Brother Gregory's Alphabet Chant shown in the library on pages 18-19.

If you match the notes from there with the ones on Herman's music, a message is revealed:

Go nine paces N(orth) and ten paces E(ast).

Pages 30-31

Their route through the labyrinth is shown in red.

Pages 32-33

The three missing things have been circled.

Pages 34-35

This is their route across the courtyard.

Pages 36-37

The spider doorway is the exit they must take.

Nerlym told Martha and Haley on page 14 that Nastina only had power over three things.

The rhyme to make the labyrinth appear (page 30) tells you what the three things are: serpents, stone and steel. Three of the doorways show serpents, steel spikes and crumbling stone steps.

Nerlym said anything else was an illusion, so Haley realizes that the spider and his web are not really there.

Pages 38-39

The Moon Goblet is here, in Hamalot's Burger Bar, being used to hold straws.

Pages 40-41

The Dark Dark Knight has been circled. He's Sir Jack Upall, who has just appeared from nowhere.

He was seen on the very first page when Haley and Martha arrived in Hamalot Castle. But he hasn't been seen since.

When Nerlym went around the castle collecting knights, he was the only knight who wasn't there.

Finally, there was one other clue to the Dark Dark Knight's identity. Haley and Martha didn't mention it. Did you spot it?

This edition first published in 2005 by Usborne Publishing Ltd., 83-85 Saffron Hill, London, EC1N 8RT. www.usborne.com